There weren't many people at the fair yet, so the workers who ran the game booths had plenty of time to notice us and try to get us to play their game.

"You have to be careful," Sonya warned me. "Some of these games are rigged. You just can't win!"

Suddenly we saw a stand with stuffed gorillas hanging from the ceiling. They had scraggly fur that looked like it was real.

"Oh, Sonya," I shouted. "Look at their faces! They're so sweet. I want to win one of those!"

Sonya couldn't believe her eyes! "I've never seen those here before. Let's see what it takes to win one."

The man running the game made it sound easy enough. . . .

Gorilla on the Midway

A TABITHA SARAH BIGBEE BOOK

BY WENDY LORD

Chariot Books™
David C. Cook Publishing Co.

IT'S A
FLIP
BOOK!

. . . .

Chariot Books™ is an imprint of David C. Cook Publishing Co.
David C. Cook Publishing Co., Elgin, Illinois 60120
David C. Cook Publishing Co., Weston, Ontario
Nova Distribution Ltd., Newton Abbot, England

GORILLA ON THE MIDWAY
© 1994 by Wendy Lord

Scripture is quoted from The Living Bible, © 1971, Tyndale House Publishers, Wheaton, IL 60189. Used by permission.

Designed by Cheryl Blum
Cover illustration by Paul Casale
Internal illustrations by Kate Flanagan
First Printing, 1994
Printed in the United States of America
98 97 96 95 94 5 4 3 2 1

Library of Congress Cataloging-in-Publication Data
Lord, Wendy.
Gorilla on the midway / by Wendy Lord.
p.   cm.
Summary: Tabitha wants a best friend so badly that she ignores her better judgment—and what she knows Jesus wants her to do—and enters her pet rabbit in the county fair, where she narrowly avoids disaster.
ISBN 0-7814-0892-X
[1. Friendship—Fiction. 2. Christian life—Fiction. 3. Rabbits—Fiction. 4. Fairs—Fiction. 5. Strangers—Fiction.] I. Title.
PZ7.L8785Go   1994
[Fic]—dc20   93-1051
                                                                    CIP
                                                                    AC

Contents

This book is for you
if you have ever been hurt
or scared by a stranger.

The Lord bless you and keep you;
The Lord make His face shine upon you;
And give you peace forever.
Amen

Children, obey your parents; this is the
right thing to do because God has placed them
in authority over you. Honor your father and
mother. This is the first of God's Ten
Commandments that ends with a promise.
And this is the promise: that if you honor your
father and mother, yours will be
a long life, full of blessing.
Ephesians 6:1-3

The Most Beautiful Girl in the World

My name is Tabitha Sarah Bigbee. I have a brand-new skateboard that I worked all summer to earn. I have a gorgeous red rabbit named Androcles who was the reason it took me all summer to earn the money for my skateboard. And I have a terrific family that includes my dad and mom, Grammy, and me. But I don't have a best friend.

The fact that I need a best friend is the only reason I agreed to go to the rabbit club meeting. There were tons of reasons not to go. First of all, Gerta Sorenson would be there.

Mrs. Sorenson is Mom's friend, and

7

she's the one who told us about the rabbit club and the show at the county fair. She offered to help me get Androcles ready to enter in the fair, but I can't stand to be around her. She always talks like she's out of breath and I hate it. It makes me nervous to talk to someone who has to work so hard to breathe. I mean, what if she stops or something?

Second, I don't want to enter Androcles in a contest. The judges will look her over and pick out all her faults. I think she's perfect. I don't want to know what a rabbit expert thinks of her.

But Grammy convinced me that maybe I would meet someone who had a rabbit like mine, and we could be best friends.

So I went to the rabbit club meeting.

And that's when Sonya Strayer came into my life.

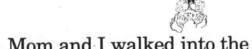

Mom and I walked into the room expecting to see a ton of rabbits, but there were only

8

people, and mostly grown-ups at that. We weren't sure we were in the right place until Mrs. Sorenson gushed over to us, full of excitement and out of breath as usual.

"Marilyn! Tabitha! How lovely! How perfectly lovely! Come sit over here by me. We're just about to start."

A man started the meeting, but they didn't talk about rabbits. They argued for fifteen minutes about whether or not they should use club money to buy new cages for someone whose barn had burned down.

A man in coveralls stood up behind me to speak. "The constitution allows for unbudgeted expenditures if the vote passes by a two-thirds majority."

I pulled Mom down to my level and whispered, "What did he say?"

"He means it's okay to use club money as long as two-thirds of the members agree."

"Mom, we studied the Constitution in school, but I didn't think it had anything to do with rabbit club money."

9

"He didn't mean the U.S. Constitution," Mom said. "He meant the rabbit club constitution. It's the set of rules they have all agreed to go by. It serves the same purpose, though."

By then they were voting. I felt pretty sorry for the lady who had lost all her rabbits, so I stuck up my hand.

Mom grabbed my arm and pulled it down. "We can't vote," she said. "We're not members."

I heard a giggle behind me. Someone was probably making fun of me for trying to vote. I slid down in my seat a little.

Then I heard another giggle, and "PSST!"

I turned around, expecting to see some kid sticking out her tongue. But there was the most beautiful girl in the world, smiling at me! She had gorgeous big blue eyes and shiny blonde braids that went almost to her waist.

She was smiling so big and her eyes were so twinkly, it made me giggle too.

10

Dear Jesus, I thought. *Could You make her my friend? Please? It would be great to have a best friend who's so pretty.*

When I finally got a chance to talk to her, I had my mouth full of Oreos. We were standing at the refreshment table after the meeting.

"Hi! I'm Sonya Strayer. What's your name?"

"Shtafisha," I managed. I quickly washed the cookie down with punch and tried again.

"Sorry. I'm Tabitha Sarah Bigbee. Do you have a rabbit?"

"Yep! He's a blue dwarf named Dopey. He's got pretty small ears for a rabbit, but he has big ears for a Netherland dwarf, so I named him Dopey, like in *Snow White*."

"I've never seen a blue rabbit," I said.

Sonya giggled again. Her eyes absolutely sparkled when she laughed. "He's not really blue. He's dark gray, but they call it blue."

Mom came up behind us with another lady. "Oh, Tabitha, I see you've already met Sonya. This is her mother, Regina Strayer. She works at the fabric store, and she was in my quilting class last year. But I never knew she raised rabbits."

Mrs. Strayer nodded. "Well, raising rabbits is only one of the too many things I do. We don't live very far from here. Would you like to see them?"

When Sonya opened the door to her garage, there were rows of stacked-up cages filled with totally black rabbits who were all as big as Androcles.

"Ohhhh!" I squealed. "They're just like Androcles! Only she's red. But they're so huge! I thought you said you had a dwarf."

"I do!" Sonya laughed. "Look over here. This is Tar-Baby and her family." She opened a cage and shoved a pile of silky black rabbits to one side.

"And this is Dopey!" There squeezed against the black mother was a small gray bundle. Sonya picked him up and handed him to me.

"A guy at the club raises these blue dwarfs," Sonya said. "He noticed that they make very nervous mothers. But our black satins are good mothers. So he tried an experiment. Tar-Baby had bunnies the same time one of his rabbits did. So he put little Dopey in with Tar-Baby, and she never noticed the difference. Now Dopey thinks

13

he's a black satin. He's just as calm as his foster brothers and sisters, even though they're three times as big as he is!"

I stroked the little rabbit in my hands. "Are you going to enter him in the fair?" I asked.

Sonya giggled and nodded, her braids bouncing up and down. "Yep. I already filled out the form."

She ran over to a metal box on a table and pulled out a piece of paper. "See here? It says 'Dopey. SS1.' That's his identification number. Then here it says 'Junior Buck, Netherland Dwarf.'

"That's all you have to do. And it only costs a dollar. Why don't you enter Androcles?"

So that's how it happened that Androcles and I got to the county fair, and how I began to learn the hard way about outside beauty and inside beauty.

The Hardest Ramp I Ever Met

Grammy made a funny little grunt when Daddy lifted her out of the car.

"Does it hurt, Mom?" he asked.

"Oh, my leg is fine! It's just that all my other body parts ache from too much inactivity."

"Well, you mind and start slowly," my mother said. "We don't want you falling and breaking anything else."

I held the front door open for them. We never used the front door before, but we do now because there are no back steps. The kitchen door opens into thin air!

The back steps we used to have were old and rotten. Grammy leaned against the railing without thinking, fell, and broke her leg.

Now we use the front door because while Grammy was in the hospital, Daddy ripped the whole back porch right off the house. I guess he felt guilty for not having fixed the railing. He had this really fierce look on his face and made a little proclamation. "Now there will be no more accidents, and I'll be forced to put new steps on!"

He pushed the kitchen table in front of the door so no one would forget and go out that way by mistake.

So now Grammy was home from the hospital, the construction crew was coming tomorrow to start building the new porch, Saturday was the opening day of the fair, and then after the fair, school started. I'd hardly had a chance to get used to my new skateboard. I was hoping we'd have a nice long fall before the snow came.

Dad laid Grammy on the sofa. She immediately sat up and started scratching our dog Everett, who was making sure Grammy knew how much he had missed her.

"Really, Richard. I'm fine. I feel strong, and if you're going to insist I lay on the sofa, I'll just go back to the hospital. At least there I had some freedom!"

Mom called from the kitchen. "Well if you feel up to peeling vegetables, I could use some help with this soup."

Grammy grabbed her crutches, and in no time at all she was in the kitchen, where she loved to be.

Grammy's always lived with us, or rather we've lived with her. She was born in this house, and since I don't have any brothers or sisters, she and I are very close.

After lunch it was the two of us doing dishes just like before, but I made her sit in a chair to dry them.

"Grammy," I said, handing her the big

17

soup pot, "it was really weird not having you around here."

"Was it really?" Grammy seemed surprised. "I was hardly gone a week! I was hoping it would give you and your mom some time alone together."

"Oh, it did. We did everything together. But I'm just used to you, that's all."

Grammy finished drying the pot and gave it back to me to put away. "I really like being with you, Tabitha. I've taken care of you ever since you were born."

"You mean because Mom was sick, right?"

"Right. And when she finally got better and came home, well, I guess I had a hard time giving you back. But you know, I might not always be here. You need to get closer to your mom now, before I'm suddenly gone and you realize you hardly even know her."

"Oh, Gram, you're not going to die! You always tell me 'Sixty isn't old, you know.' "

"Well, I'm not ready to die," Gram said,

18

"but maybe I'm ready for a change. I've always lived here. I never thought of leaving because I was useful here. But you're growing up, and you all did quite well without me while I was in the hospital."

I couldn't believe what I was hearing. "But why, Grammy? Where would you go?"

"Oh, don't worry. I haven't made any plans. I'm just sort of open to the idea, that's all. As for why . . . do you realize that I'm sleeping in the very bed I was born in? That's reason enough right there."

I stood there, staring at Grammy until she said to me, "Tabitha, the phone's ringing."

I shook Grammy's new ideas out of my head and ran to answer the phone.

It was Sonya.

"Hi. I'm at Mrs. Sorenson's. She wants to know if you're putting Androcles in the sanctioned show or the exhibition or both."

"Well, I don't know. What's the difference?"

Sonya sighed. I guess she thought I didn't know anything! "The sanctioned

19

show is where they judge the animals in each class and give them points for different stuff, like their fur and weight. If they are a lot like their breed is supposed to be, they get more points.

"The exhibition is just a display," Sonya went on. "The rabbits stay there all week for people to look at, but no one judges them."

The exhibition sounded more like what I'd like. So I told her to enter me only in that part. "I really hate the idea of hearing all about Androcles's faults," I told her.

"Okay, then just tell me her registration number."

"She doesn't have one yet. I thought the people at the fair would do that."

"She'll get a fair number when we get there, but I mean the number on her ear."

"She hasn't got one."

"Well, never mind, I'll just make something up. My mom has a gadget that will do it. I'll see if we can bring it over. Boy, I

20

wish I lived near you. I haven't even seen Androcles yet!"

After she hung up, I got to thinking how much nicer it would be if Sonya lived next to us instead of Jason Harrington. But she probably wouldn't have a skateboard ramp.

And I planned to spend the rest of the afternoon getting used to Jason's new mini-ramp.

The ramp was shaped something like a giant letter U. There was a platform at the top of each side, and the sides were taller than me. The idea was to start on one platform, which was up against the hill in Jason's backyard, swoop down into the curve of the ramp, and get enough force to make it up to the other platform.

You needed to pump your legs just the right amount at just the right spot to make it up there, and so far, neither Jason nor I could manage it. In fact, we rarely managed to stay on our boards.

I knew what I was in for, by practicing at Jason's. Probably two hours of, "Hey, Tabitha, watch this!"

But I got to Jason's just in time to see a great demonstration of not staying on your board.

"Are you okay?" I called.

Jason didn't answer. Instead, he picked himself up off the plywood bottom of the ramp and scrambled up the hill to the platform. "Watch this!"

I had to admit that even when Jason wasn't good at something, he never let that change his opinion of himself.

"Boy, Tabitha, I don't know why they call this thing a mini-ramp. It seems like it's forty miles high. They ought to call it a Super U. Or Super Impossible!"

Jason was right, for once. "Mini-ramp" was a dumb thing to call it. From up on the platform it looked like a mountain, or rather, the valley between two mountains.

22

I stood at the top of the ramp with my board and looked at the valley below. I was determined to practice until I got it. Finally, I decided just to go for it. I swooped down into the flat bottom and up the other side. But the only part of me that made it to the other platform was my chin. It slammed hard on the edge with the weight of my whole body behind it. I let out a wail, and slid down into the bottom of the ramp.

23

·3·

··

The Once-in-a-Lifetime Opportunity

Yikes! Mom, that stings! I want Grammy to do it!"

"Tabitha, hold still, please. It's not me that's stinging you. It's the disinfectant. Just let me get this cleaned off, then we can get the ointment on it.

"There. Now how's that?"

I was trying hard to stop the tears. "It still hurts."

Mom kissed the top of my head. "I know, honey. It's badly bruised. Thank God you still have all your teeth, and you didn't even bite your tongue!"

24

"Mom, it's not fair. I was wearing a helmet and knee pads and elbow pads. But I hit the platform with my face. Even if I was wearing a body cast I still would have gotten hurt!"

Mom laughed. "Imagine how that would look, skating in a body cast!"

"With a bandage on my chin," I grumped.

Mom gave me a little shove toward the living room. "Go sit with Grammy for a while. I made her take a break, and she looks lonely."

After Grammy inspected my beat-up chin, I inspected her toes sticking out of her cast.

"They still look sort of purple, Grammy. You'd better keep them propped up awhile." I rubbed her toes a little and tried not to tickle her.

"Grammy, I want Sonya to be my best friend, but how will I know if she is?"

Grammy thought a minute. "Is she the friend who you like the best?"

"Well, not really. I mean, I don't really

know her. She doesn't go to my school, and she doesn't live near me. You can't have a best friend if you never see her."

Grammy smiled. "I haven't seen my best friend for forty-two years."

"Then how can you be friends?"

"We've been writing letters since high school, and we talk on the phone every now and then."

"You mean Etta Chapman?"

Grammy shifted her weight and moved her leg into a better position. "That's right! Her family moved away during our last year of high school. We wrote a lot at first because she was so terribly lonely. She intended to come back here as soon as she finished school, but she met a fellow and got married instead. I've shown you pictures of her granddaughters."

"Yeah, you get a letter from Montana practically every other week! But how can you be friends if you can't do things together?"

"You know, Tabitha, that's the funny thing. We didn't do things together even when we were in school. Not really. We didn't like to do the same things, and we didn't have the same abilities.

"But down inside where it really counts," Grammy continued, "that's where we're friends. Soul mates, Etta and I are. We have helped each other trust God through

27

all the tough times in our lives, and we have rejoiced together through all the happy times."

"Is she beautiful?"

Grammy looked at me. "What? Oh . . . I don't know. I never really thought about it. I don't suppose so. She's pleasant looking, though. And she's beautiful on the inside."

"What do you mean, Gram?"

"Well, on the outside, it's just a person's body that's beautiful. But a person who's beautiful on the inside has a good heart. That's the kind of beauty that really counts. Fortunately for us, God loves us whether we're beautiful or not, inside or out. And He can make our insides beautiful if we let Him."

I got up and touched my sore chin gingerly. "Well, I don't know Sonya's inside yet. But on the outside she is the most beautiful girl in the world. She's got blonde hair down to her waist, and it's French braided with ribbons IN the braids, not just at the ends. Her

28

eyes are so sparkly. When she smiles she just makes you want to smile too."

"Sounds like she could be a good friend, if she makes you smile. You'll have to look for an opportunity to get to know her better."

I found that opportunity later that afternoon when Sonya called, again.

"Tabitha, are you going to stay at the fair, or are you going to come in every day?"

"We usually only come once, like on family night or half-price day."

Sonya seemed shocked. "Tabitha, you have to be there every day to take care of your rabbit. Nobody does it for you, you know!"

"I guess I didn't think about that part of it," I mumbled. "Do you have to pay at the gate every day, just to go in and feed your rabbit?"

"No, silly. They give you a pass. But never mind. My mom has a booth where she sells her dried flowers and baskets. We'll be staying on the grounds in our camper. Tell your mom you can just stay with us."

Now that wasn't something I could just go "tell my mom." What followed was quite a bit of discussion and lots of phone calls, but finally all that was left was to talk with Daddy at supper.

"So," Mom was saying, "we ended up making a deal that we'd bring half the groceries, and I'd get supper for the girls and take something over to Regina at her booth. She's got to be there from 11 a.m. to 11 p.m. Then she's going home."

"Mrs. Strayer says she can't sleep in the camper," I said, "especially after working at the booth all day. She's got a bad back."

Daddy winked at me. "It may be having two little girls in the camper that makes it hard for her to sleep."

"Don't worry," Mom said. "I'll keep them in line. We've talked about the rules."

"Right." I said. I figured I'd better recite the rules to prove I had been listening. "We have to stay together whenever we leave the rabbit house or the camping area. We have to ask before we go on the . . . what's it called where the games and rides are?"

"The midway," Mom said.

"Right. We have to ask first and stay together. You always have to know where we are. Never touch anyone else's animal, and there's a quiet rule on the whole fairgrounds after midnight. Oh, and we're never allowed on the midway after dark."

Daddy raised his eyebrows. "Sounds like you have that all down pat! But, Marilyn, what about your sewing business? Can you afford a week off?"

"I'm in kind of a lull right now. I only have one wedding coming up at Christmas. There's a lot of embroidery to be done on that dress, which I can do at the fair. Regina said I can sit down in the camping area, or right up at the booth with her. I can even

31

put my business cards out on her table. This week off may end up bringing in new orders for me."

Mom took a deep breath. "And I get a vacation at the fair in her camper, and Tabitha and Sonya can be there to look after their rabbits."

Grammy served me some more spaghetti. "Have you got any money, Tabitha?"

"Sure," I said. "I've got nine dollars. Maybe even ten if you count the change."

"Well," Daddy said, "I'll give you fifteen, which will include your allowance for the next two weeks. That's almost twenty-five dollars total. Think you can spend that in a week?"

Mom looked me right in the eye. "But when it's gone, it's gone. Period. You can spend it all the first day if you're not careful!"

"Well, Miss Tabitha," Daddy said, "how many kids ever get to live at the fair? This is really a once-in-a-lifetime opportunity. You can thank God for a friend like Sonya."

"I think so too," I said. "And I'll really get to know her, if I'm living with her!"

Daddy said to Grammy, "Mom, with you down here in the guest room, I guess you won't have too much trouble while I'm at work. Do you think Betsy Harmon will look in on you once in a while?"

Grammy laughed. "I'm sure of it. She's already called me three times today!"

Daddy seemed satisfied with the plan. "Looks like Gram and I can manage here alone. I'm going to do the finishing work on the new back porch next week after work. It will be a good time for you to be gone."

"Speaking of the new porch," Grammy said, "what time will they be here in the morning?"

"Seven o'clock," Dad turned and grinned at me, "so don't go out to let the chickens out wearing your pajamas!"

"Oh, Daddy," I said, "I never let the chickens wear my pajamas!"

33

I got him that time. Daddy always tries to mix up people's words. When I was little, I would ask something like, "Would you please put my mittens on?" And he would stand there and try to get them on himself! Then he'd look surprised when I said I wanted them on me! But this time I beat him at his own game.

While Grammy and I were doing the dishes that night, I noticed a silly grin on her face.

"What are you so smiley about?" I asked.

"I'm smiling because the Lord answers prayer. He's a good God who listens to us."

I rinsed a handful of silverware and plopped it in the drainer. "What do you mean, Gram?"

"Well," she said, "I've been praying for a way for you to get to know Sonya better. But I never expected anything like this. There is just no better way. When you live with someone, you get to know their character, their inside right away. God knows you're

34

serious about wanting a best friend, and it looks as if He's got something up His sleeve."

"I hope it's something good."

Grammy got really serious. "Tabitha, that's one thing you must always remember. Whatever God has planned is always good, even if it's not pleasant, or what you expected."

Well, what eventually happened at the fair was not pleasant, and certainly not what I expected. I had to think hard and long to figure out how it was good.

·4·

....

The Most Major Minor Surgery

Friday turned out to be one of the busiest, wildest days I can remember. The carpenters had already been hammering and sawing with an incredibly loud electric saw for an hour before I even had my breakfast.

When I went out to let out the chickens, the workers already had a lot of the frame up. You couldn't quite tell what it was going to be yet, but I was impressed by how fast they worked!

Mom went to town and shopped for groceries for the week, and I packed my clothes.

She was struggling in with the bags just

as I came down the stairs with my suitcase.

"Did you pack your raincoat?"

"Oh, Mom, I hate that raincoat."

"Tabitha, usually if it rains we just don't go to the fair that day. But this year we won't have a choice. It could rain all week, and the fairgrounds could turn into Mud Lake."

She turned around to put some things in the refrigerator. "Pack the raincoat. If you argue, I'll make you take your boots, too."

I packed the raincoat.

Then I went outside to pack Androcles. The fair didn't start till tomorrow, but the animals had to be there today. Someone from the rabbit club would help us check in, but I had to bring everything Androcles needed.

I put her bag of food inside a big plastic bag, in case it spilled. Then I got two one-gallon jugs and filled them with our water. I thought they might have different-tasting water at the fair, and I didn't want to take any chances that Androcles wouldn't like it.

Then I got a couple chunks of wood, so she'd have something to chew on. I didn't think she was going to like being in a cage all week.

At the last minute, I took off my old sweatshirt and threw that in the chicken crate that was Androcles's travel cage. I figured she would like having something that smelled familiar in a strange place.

Back in the house Mom was busily cutting out the last pieces of the wedding dress that she wanted to take along.

"Wouldn't it be awful if you dropped that in Mud Lake, Mom?"

"Don't worry. I've thought of that. I'm going to wrap it well. We'll be camping with all the 4-H kids and their animals. I don't imagine it will be too pleasant underfoot even if it doesn't rain."

"I wouldn't want you to make my wedding dress at the fair. It might smell like a cow barn or something."

"Stop, please! Don't put worries in my

head. It's too full already. If you're done packing, why don't you go down and see Jason. The Strayers will be here right after lunch."

On my way to Jason's, I stopped to see how the porch was coming along. Was it ever!

The carpenters were doing much more hammering than sawing now. And it looked like a porch. The boards of the roof were almost all on, but you couldn't tell yet where the windows were going to be.

Since we were leaving for the fair today, I wasn't going to get to see them finish it. But that was okay with me. I would rather go to the fair, stay with Sonya, and get her for a friend. Maybe even a best friend.

But now I had two hours on my skateboard before lunch. That is, if I could stay off my face.

Well, I couldn't believe it, and neither could Jason, but I actually stayed on my feet!

I had decided to stop trying to make it up to the other platform, until I got used to keeping my balance on the board. I spent most of the time just rocking back and forth in the curve of the mini-ramp. I experimented with pumping my legs and seeing how far I could go.

"Tabitha, you have good balance," Jason said. "Anytime I pump, or move at all, I fall off."

"Thanks," I said, a little surprised at a compliment from Jason. "I'm going to try to make it one more time before I go home. I think I've got the hang of pumping now."

"You should! That's all you've been doing!"

I took off down the ramp, and just as I came out of the bottom, I pumped hard and . . .

Well, yes, I stumbled, and no, it wasn't graceful, but I made it. I was on the platform and so was my board!

For a minute I just stood there drinking

in the feeling of winning. Yes! This was good! For just a moment, I forgot that I had plain brown hair. I forgot that I had a huge bruise and a cut on my chin. I forgot that I wouldn't be able to skate again for a whole week.

But back at my house, I remembered.

Sonya got out of the car with her blonde hair in a huge puffy ponytail. The long

41

ends of it were brought up to the rubber band and fastened with a blue bow that exactly matched her eyes. She flashed her sparkly blue eyes at me and said, "What did you do to your chin? It looks terrible!"

"I fell on the skateboard ramp."

"Skateboard! Yuk! Only boys do that." Then she gave her ponytail a flip and said, "Show me Androcles."

When Sonya saw my rabbit, she squealed, "Oh, she's gorgeous!"

Maybe Sonya and I were soul mates after all.

Suddenly she got real busy. "Okay, Tabitha, we have to hurry. We want to get the good hutches. They have to be near the front so everyone can see our rabbits, but not near the door, because you don't want the drafts and rain. Where's her traveling cage?"

Sonya didn't say anything about the chicken crate. Maybe it wasn't so out of the ordinary, or maybe she was just trying to

42

be polite. But she pulled the sweatshirt out and tossed it aside.

"Wait," I said, "I put that in there on purpose. I want her to have something that smells like me so she won't get so upset."

Sonya started to laugh, but her eyes didn't sparkle this time. I guess it depends on the light. "What's the matter?" she said in a whiny voice. "Does she need her blanky?"

"Yes!"

Deep in my heart I prayed that Sonya would never discover the "blanky" that was tucked inside my sleeping bag. I haven't really needed it for years. It's just that I sleep better away from home if it's with me.

I put Androcles in the chicken crate, and Sonya carried it to the back of the station wagon. Mom was there putting in our sleeping bags and the suitcases. She pointed to Sonya's little gray Dopey in his tiny traveling hutch.

"Only one?" she asked. "I thought you'd

bring the whole tribe!"

Mrs. Strayer nodded. "Harold's bringing them all in Sunday morning when the judges are there. Wait till you see all the rabbits. They come in every shape and size from all over Maine and even parts of Canada. Luckily, most of them go home as soon as they're judged, and by evening, the rabbit house is back to normal. Only the exhibition rabbits stay all week."

Mom brought the groceries from the house.

"Is that it?" Mrs. Strayer asked. "Are we ready?"

But Sonya was checking Androcles. "Mom, I forgot. Tabitha's rabbit needs a tattoo. Did you bring your thing?"

"Sure. It'll just take a minute." Mrs. Strayer started digging around in a box.

I wasn't sure I had heard right. "A tattoo?"

Sonya's voice was very snappy. I guess she got tired of explaining things to me. Maybe I shouldn't ask so many questions.

44

"Tabitha, I told you all rabbits need an identification number in their ear."

"I know," I said. "But I thought it was just ink. I didn't know it was . . . permanent!"

Mrs. Strayer pulled a terrible-looking object out of the box. "Permanent is the whole idea," she said. "That way breeders can keep track of things, and everyone gets their own rabbits back at the end of the fair. You wouldn't want someone else to claim your rabbit, would you?"

"No . . . but won't it hurt?"

"I promise," Mrs. Strayer laughed, "you won't feel a thing! It's really very minor surgery!"

Mom stopped me for a moment. "Tabitha, you don't have to have her tattooed. We don't have to go to the fair. But if she goes, she goes with a tattoo."

"Okay, but I don't have to watch. I'll be inside saying good-bye to Grammy." And pretending this isn't happening, I added to myself.

45

When they called me out again, I ran right over to inspect Androcles. There on the inside of her beautiful red ear was a permanently ugly tattoo that said "TB1."

TB1! How awful. I didn't want her branded with my initials. Now everyone would know that I let it happen. I couldn't pretend she was that way when I got her.

"Look!" I hollered. "She's bleeding!"

Sonya said in a very grown-up voice, "No, she's not, Tabitha. Look again. It's just a little red and puffy. Believe me, in five minutes she won't even notice it. And neither will you."

I timed it. Five minutes later I still had tears in my eyes and Androcles was still pulling at her ear. No one else even noticed.

The Most Rabbits Ever

I felt like a movie star, driving up to the exhibitors' gate, flashing our blue passes, and getting waved right through!

This time, we wouldn't have to go home when our money ran out! We were going to live here! And it would be just Sonya and me. Maybe we'd have a real chance to turn into best friends.

On the way to the fairgrounds, I had slowly gotten over Androcles's major minor surgery. I guess she did too, because she was just sitting in her chicken crate looking regular.

I don't think she realized that her week was going to be different than usual, until

47

we unloaded her crate at the rabbit house. Then she woke up!

She sniffed and ran around in circles, then she sniffed some more.

"Really, Androcles, you're as bad as some old dog. In fact you look just like Everett when you do that! You can probably smell more rabbits here than you ever knew existed."

Sonya set Dopey's cage down next to Androcles's. "There," she said, scratching his fur through the wire, "you two get to know each other. We'll get you hutches right beside each other. The redheaded giant and the little blue dwarf. That sounds like the name of a fairy tale." Then she turned to me, and smiled. "Come on, Tabby. Let's get them signed in."

I went with her, and ignored the fact that she called me Tabby. Usually I hate being called anything but Tabitha. But maybe a best friend had a right to give you a nickname.

Anyway, right now there was too much going on to think about it.

There were several cages left in the first section, but only one in the front row. Since Dopey was so much smaller than Androcles, he needed the one in the front.

So instead of side by side, they ended up in hutches back to back, but they could still see each other and even touch noses through the wire.

I didn't see any other red satins yet. I'm glad I took Androcles. She really is a special-looking rabbit. Mrs. Sorenson had said there weren't many red satins besides Androcles in this area. Maybe she would know if any others were entered in the exhibit.

But Gerta Sorenson and her breathing problem were nowhere around.

"She's in Connecticut," Sonya's mother said. "Her daughter just had a baby. I guess babies are more important than bunnies, even to Mrs. Sorenson."

"Thank You, God," I breathed to myself,

although it probably wasn't polite to be thankful for something like that.

Sonya showed me all the black satins like the ones she and her parents raised.

"The two-color ones over there are called Dutch, but I like these lop-ears best."

She took me to a hutch with the saddest looking bunnies. "What makes their ears hang down that way?"

Sonya shrugged. "It's just the way they are. Nobody does anything to them."

Suddenly I noticed a family of small gray rabbits next to us. "Look, Sonya, these gray ones are even smaller than Dopey. And look at this baby. He's as tiny as a mouse!"

A man's voice sounded behind us. "Then I'll name him Mighty Mouse."

We wheeled around to find a short, round-faced man in green coveralls. I'd seen him before at the rabbit club meeting. He was the man who knew all about the constitution.

"Hi, Mr. Rusk!" Sonya squealed. "I

thought these blues belonged to you. Are they some of Dopey's family?"

Mr. Rusk yanked on Sonya's ponytail and winked at me. "No, Dopey's line all have great fur and great bones, but I could never get them small enough. They were always way overweight! And such big ears! They're only good for the stewpot."

I winced, but Mr. Rusk didn't seem to

51

notice. He reached in and picked up the tiniest bunny.

"Now these! These I've bred smaller and smaller with each generation. If little Mighty Mouse here is tough enough to make it, he will be a good buck to keep my dwarfs small."

I looked with alarm at the tiny animal who sat quivering in Mr. Rusk's hand. "Why would he need to be tough? Is he all right?"

Mr. Rusk put Mighty Mouse back and rearranged some of the bunnies. "Oh, he's just so little that the bigger ones push him out of the way sometimes. He might not be getting enough to eat."

"If he were mine, I'd feed him with an eyedropper until he was big enough to fight."

Mr. Rusk smiled. "I've got seventy-six rabbits, honey. I just don't have time to do that."

I stared at him in amazement. "Seventy-six! I had ten red satins this summer, and that kept me busy enough. I can't imagine seventy-six."

Sonya bounced up and down. "Once we had two hundred and twenty!" But Mr. Rusk was still looking at me.

"Red satins, huh? Then that nice-looking doe over there must be yours," he said, pointing over at Androcles.

I started to tell him about how I found Androcles, and about her babies, but Sonya grabbed his arm.

"Come see how big Dopey is now! You'll be surprised." While Mr. Rusk was making a fuss over Dopey, Mrs. Strayer stuck her head in the door of the rabbit house.

"There you are, girls. Come on! I'll show you where the camper is."

I don't know what I was expecting when I thought of a camper. Maybe a tent on wheels. But Sonya's camper was huge! And nicer inside than our house!

"Mom!" I shrieked. "Look at this bathroom! It has a shower and everything!"

But Mom was checking out the kitchen. There was a gas stove, and a refrigerator, and cupboards and drawers in every little corner. The kitchen sink had a flip-down dish rack that tucked away into the wall.

The living room area even had a sofa and TV! The driver's seat and the other front seat turned completely around into the living room like easy chairs.

All we had to do to "set up camp" was put our groceries away and hang up our clothes. Then we helped Mrs. Strayer get all her baskets and flower arrangements out of the camper and load them into the station wagon.

"I'll take these up to my booth. Why don't you three walk up there and meet me? There's not an extra square inch in the car!"

We passed a huge tent set up on a grassy area, where a lady with fluffy white hair was exercising three big poodles. The sign beside the tent said "Trixie's Trick Dogs.

54

FREE Shows every day at 12 noon, 2 p.m., and 4 p.m. Rancko the Singing Magician. FREE Shows at 11 a.m., 1 p.m., and 3 p.m."

"Well," Mom laughed, "between Trixie and Rancko, you shouldn't lack for something to do during the day!"

It sure was strange walking through the midway before the fair opened. I knew I was privileged to be allowed in there. Workers were everywhere setting up rides and tents.

"Mom, do you know what's missing here?" I asked.

"What?"

"Trash! There's no trash on the ground! Usually this place looks like a dump."

Sonya giggled and bounced her ponytail. "Yep! That's why I'm so glad we have a camper with a bathroom. The rest rooms here are gross! You should have seen last year. . . ."

But Mom stopped her just in time, and we turned into the exhibition hall.

When we found Mrs. Strayer, she was surrounded by three frantic men, and she was practically having a fit!

"I paid for and reserved this corner space a whole year in advance. And you've let these water heaters in here."

"They're not water heaters, ma'am. They're water softeners."

"I don't care if they're water lilies! They're in my space."

There was silence for a few seconds. I wondered if everyone was as embarrassed as I was.

A man with a clipboard said, "But he needs more electrical outlets than you will, and I didn't want to overload that circuit up there. Can't I put you between the snowmobiles?"

Mrs. Strayer just glared.

"Okay. Move the water softeners. I'll have Jack run another line from somewhere else." He shook his head and walked away.

Mrs. Strayer slumped down into a

folding chair. Then all at once, she slapped her knees and popped up like nothing ever happened.

"You get one table and two chairs with this space. The rest you have to do yourself. Wait till you see the setup Harold made me."

She came back from the car with a flat thing about as big as an ironing board. But unfolded, it was a beautiful pale blue wall with holes all through it. She snapped some legs onto the bottom edge of the wall and stood it up behind her table.

"I'll get the pegs!" Sonya called, and raced off to the car.

She and I got to put the little pegs in all the holes, while Mom and Mrs. Strayer unpacked the flower arrangements from the boxes.

By the time we got back to the rabbit house, every cage was full.

"See," Sonya said, "I told you it was good to get here early. Dopey is so special, he needs to be in a good place so everyone can see him."

"Androcles too," I said.

"Yeah," said Sonya. "Tabitha, if you think there are a lot of rabbits in here now, wait till Sunday. There'll be cages stacked everywhere, and hardly space to walk."

Sonya was right about Sunday! Dad came and got Mom and me real early Sunday morning so we could get to church and help Grammy get ready in time. The rabbit house was still and quiet when we left.

But when we pulled back into the fairgrounds, it looked like it had been raining rabbits for a week.

58

·6·

The Best of Breed Indeed

Sonya practically attacked me when I got out of the car.

"Tabitha, where have you been?"

"At church," I said.

Sonya looked at me like I was crazy. "Tabby, nobody should have to go to church on fair day!"

"Sonya, please don't call me Tabby. And anyway, we don't have to go, we just always do. It sort of helps you get the week started right. Know what I mean?"

Sonya did not know what I meant. She stared at me a minute and then shrugged. "Never mind. Come on!"

We picked our way carefully through a

maze of station wagons and pickup trucks, and little cages and boxes stacked on the ground outside the rabbit house. I saw now why Sonya didn't notice that Androcles's "traveling cage" was a chicken crate.

Rabbits were arriving in every kind of container imaginable. Most of them were in some kind of real wire cage or hutch. But some were in chicken crates, or cat carriers. Some were in cardboard boxes, or picnic baskets. There was even one little bunny that came to the fair in a big Tupperware container!

The rule book only said that a traveling cage had to have a bottom in it, had to have proper ventilation, and had to be big enough for the rabbit to turn around in. I suppose a Tupperware container with holes all around it followed those rules, but it struck me funny anyway. I mean, what if you went to show your rabbit to the judge, and it turned out to be macaroni salad!

Inside the rabbit house was worse! What

little floor space there was, was taken up by two high carpeted tables that had dividers and a little box at the back of each section to keep the rabbits separate. A rabbit judge in a long white coat stood at each table.

"The judge at the other table is Avery Thompson," Sonya told me. "I hope he does Dopey. Mom says he's the best rabbit man on the East Coast. If he gives your rabbit good marks, you know you've got a good breeder."

Just then, Mr. Rusk tacked a sign up on the bulletin board, then turned around to announce to the crowd, "Mini-lops now at table one, black satins at table two as soon as the Angora's are done. Reds and dwarfs after that."

Mrs. Strayer called across the rabbit house, "Sonya! Over here."

I left them to fuss over their rabbits. They were up next, and they were going to be judged at table two by Avery Thompson, the best rabbit man on the East Coast. No wonder Sonya's parents were in such a sweat.

I went to check on my rabbit.

"Hi, Androcles," I murmured, scratching between her ears. "Here, let me fluff up your sweatshirt. I'm glad I brought this along for you.

"You know, Androcles, you really are the best-looking rabbit here. There are only two other red satins in the exhibition, and they're big ugly bucks. They look more like bulldogs than bunnies. Nobody here is as pretty or sweet as you."

"Oh, I don't know about that. I'm pretty sweet!" Dad had come up behind me.

"Hi, Dad."

"Hi, honey. Mom's gone up to the exhibition hall to look after Mrs. Strayer's booth till she's finished with the rabbit judging. But I thought I'd stay and get in the way around here."

I shut the door of the hutch and snuggled up against Daddy. "It's not hard to get in the way today, Daddy. I didn't know there were so many rabbits in the world!"

"How's it going with you and your friend?"

"Oh, okay. You couldn't exactly say we are best friends yet, but it is only Sunday. We've got six more days. After the judging is over, we'll have more time to just hang around."

We wandered down the row of hutches, stepping around rabbits and people.

The Strayers and some other people were all standing behind the judging table, reaching into the little boxes in front of them, and hanging onto silky black masses of rabbits.

"Look, Daddy. They're judging the black satins now. Do you think we can get close enough to hear without being in the way?"

Daddy and I squeezed in a little closer. Avery Thompson moved down along the table, taking each rabbit out of its little "waiting room." He turned the animal

63

around to face him, and bunched up the bunny's bottom end a little, tucking its legs underneath, and feeling its bones.

Daddy grinned. "That guy looks like he knows what he's doing. I can't tell one from the other!"

"Sonya says he's the biggest expert around."

Everyone else thought so too apparently, because no one was saying a word. Everyone around the table seemed to be concentrating to hear what the judge had to say.

He checked the rabbits all over, their eyes, the color and the quality of their fur, their body sizes and shapes, the size of their heads. He even checked their feet and toenails. And each time he would say "poor" or "fair" or "good" or "very good."

Then a kind of secretary person, sitting at the end of the table, would record his marks in a book and on a little card.

As each rabbit was finished, the owner

would collect his card from the secretary, put the rabbit back in his traveling cage, and plop another one into the little box along the back of the judge's table. It was going to take a year to get through all these rabbits one at a time.

Daddy and I went to get some lunch.

When we got back, all the black rabbits had turned into red rabbits.

"Daddy, that man has Androcles! I didn't want her in the judging!"

But Daddy held onto my hand and pointed across the room. "Look over there, Tabitha. She's still in her cage."

I looked where Dad was pointing and, of course, there was Androcles, right where she was supposed to be, cleaning her back toenails without a care in the world.

"How terrible!" I said. "I don't even know my own rabbit!"

Daddy laughed. "Why don't you stay and watch. I'm going to go find Mom."

There were only about ten red satins,

65

and they all seemed to belong to one man. He came over to me while I was checking the tattoo in Androcles's ear to make sure it said TB1.

"Does that doe belong to you, miss?"

"Yes, she does." I thought at first he was accusing me of messing with someone else's rabbit.

The man smiled. "I raise the big reds too, and she could beat my rabbits, for sure."

He handed me a little white card. "If you ever want to sell her, give me a call."

I was never going to sell Androcles. She and I had been through a lot together. This fair was a great once-in-a-lifetime opportunity, but it would be nice to get her home and get things back to normal.

Right now I had to help Sonya get through Dopey's judging. Her parents were packing up their black satins to take them home. But Sonya had Dopey in her arms wrapped in a towel, waiting for an open space at the judging table. They had just started the Netherland dwarfs.

I know I'm no expert. I mean, I didn't even recognize my own rabbit. But these dwarf bunnies were a lot smaller than Dopey, and their ears were tiny.

Dear Jesus, I thought, *please don't let them make fun of Sonya's rabbit. She thinks he's great, and maybe he is, but please make the judge think so too. And thank You that I didn't enter Androcles.*

Sonya finally found an empty slot and popped Dopey into the waiting box.

"I can't see over the boxes, Sonya. I'm going around behind the judge and watch from there."

She giggled. "Okay. Wish me luck!"

"Sure," I said. "I'll do better than that. I'll pray for you."

Sonya gave me a funny look and turned around to wait for Dopey's turn.

I worked my way to the other side of the table just in time to see Avery Thompson

pick up the little blue-gray bundle that was Dopey. He held the rabbit up in the air, turned him around, and then tucked him under his arm. His shoulders raised once and he let out a deep breath as he said, "This rabbit is not a dwarf."

Talk and noise and life itself stopped all over the rabbit house. Apparently, the Strayers, Mr. Rusk, and everyone else had thought that Dopey was a Netherland dwarf, but the EXPERT had just pronounced them wrong.

I held my breath. *Oh, dear God,* I prayed, *I told Sonya I'd pray for her, and now this happened. She'll be disqualified, and she'll think it's Your fault! Then she'll never be my friend, or Yours!*

All heads turned silently to stare at the little rabbit. Avery Thompson looked at Sonya's gorgeous face peeking up over the back of the table, her eyes sparkling—with tears this time—and her two fists clutched at her mouth.

Then he laughed and announced to the crowd, "But he's a very nice Polish! We can judge the Polish class right now . . . if no one has any objection?"

I let out my breath, and everyone laughed. Several people patted Sonya on the back or tugged at her braid. Sonya flashed her best smile at the judge.

Avery Thompson's voice was loud and

clear as he ticked off Dopey's grades. "Head, good. Eyes, very good. Ears, very good. Color, very good. The fur lacks just a little luster and shine. I'll have to give that a good. Body conformation, very good. Feet, very good."

Now the judge held up Dopey and spoke to the crowd. "I'm giving him best of breed."

Everyone laughed. Dopey was the only Polish there! Of course he was the best!

But the expert continued. "We never give ribbons to unworthy animals. It's not the policy of the Fair Association or the Rabbit Association. This rabbit may be the only one in his class, but he's getting the ribbon because he's worth it."

He carefully placed Dopey in Sonya's hands.

"Thank You, Jesus." I mumbled under my breath. "Thank You, thank You."

70

7

The Biggest Rip-off at the Fair

Well, the sanctioned show was over. All but the exhibition rabbits had gone home by Sunday evening. Androcles was all tucked in with her sweatshirt. Dopey was back in his exhibition hutch with his huge red, white, and blue ribbon hanging on the front. And Sonya, Mom, and I were snuggled up on the big bed in the back room of the camper, making plans for the rest of our week.

Sometime just after Trixie's trick dogs, I fell asleep.

71

It was light out when Sonya shook me awake. "Tabitha, it's morning. Your mom let us stay here all night. She's out on the bunk."

I groaned and turned over. I hated to get up. Having a best friend who liked to chat early in the morning was not going to be easy.

At breakfast Mom asked us what our plans were for the day. Sonya had everything worked out.

"We're going to take our turn baby-sitting the rabbit house till Mr. Rusk comes in at eleven. Then we're going to see the trick dogs and the magician and check out every game on the midway to see what we can win."

"Sounds expensive!" Mom said.

At the rabbit house, we basically just looked at the rabbits and sat there. The fair didn't officially open till eleven, so we really didn't have much to do. A few of the 4-H kids came around, but most of them

72

were busy with their own animals.

Some of those poor 4-H kids worked all morning shoveling manure, hauling straw or wood shavings, milking, washing, brushing, and exercising their animals.

"They must really like their cows!" I said to Sonya. "That's a lot of work."

"Maybe they just like the money," Sonya said. "The first-place beef last year was auctioned for more than four dollars a pound!"

Of course! It hadn't occurred to me that these animals were here for the beef auction. And after that, the stewpot!

At least Androcles was coming home with me after the fair.

Just before eleven, Sonya and I looked over all the rabbits in the exhibition again.

But the report we had for Mr. Rusk wasn't good. Mighty Mouse was sick.

"When we first came in, we thought he was just sleeping," we told him. "But now look!"

73

All the other baby bunnies were having lunch, but little Mighty Mouse was shivering in a corner all by himself.

"Mr. Rusk, he's really sick!" Sonya wailed. "His eyes are all watery, and he can hardly breathe!"

Mr. Rusk picked up the tiny rabbit, unzipped the neck of his coveralls, and put Mighty Mouse inside, in his shirt pocket.

"I'll keep him warm in there for a while. When the others are done, I'll see if he wants some milk."

"What if he won't eat?" I asked. But I already knew the answer.

Mr. Rusk patted his pocket gently. "Oh, he may come around yet. Don't worry about him."

Actually, I didn't worry about him at all the rest of the afternoon. We went back to the camper to get our money and some lunch, said good-bye to Mom, and went off to seek our fortune on the midway.

Rancko's magic show was already

over by the time we walked past the big tent, so we headed toward the midway, where good smells were starting to come from the food booths.

There weren't many people there yet, so the workers who ran the game booths had plenty of time to notice us and try to get us to play their game.

"You have to be careful," Sonya warned me. "Some of these games are rigged. Some of them you just can't win!"

Suddenly we saw a stand with stuffed gorillas hanging from the ceiling. They had scraggly fur that looked like it was real.

"Oh, Sonya," I shouted. "Look at their faces! They're so sweet. I want to win one of those!"

Sonya couldn't believe her eyes! "I've never seen those here before. Let's see what it takes to win one."

The man running the game made it sound easy enough. "Just shoot this water gun. Fill up the cup before the bell rings

and you get a collector plate. When you win five collector plates, you can turn them in for a gorilla!"

He shifted his cigar to the other cheek. "Only costs a buck to play. Get a prize just for playing."

Sonya was suspicious. "What do you mean about a prize just for playing? What if I don't fill up the cup?"

76

The man leaned down as though he were telling us some big secret. "You get a prize every time you play. Ten of them gets you a collector plate."

Sonya pulled me over to the side. "Look, the cups are fastened to the shelf, so they won't tip over. And they're tilted toward us. Maybe we can do it."

It truly was a great gorilla, not like any I had ever seen in a store.

We each paid a dollar and sat down at the water guns, which were bolted to the table. When the starting bell rang we fired away.

Even when I could hit the cup, the force of the water was so great that most of it splashed back out again. I didn't fill it up to the line before the bell rang, and neither did Sonya.

But we each got a prize. It was a mirror about the size of a sandwich with a picture of Elvis Presley on it.

8

The Grandest Gorilla Plan

When we left the stand we each had six Elvis mirrors.

Sonya made a face. "Where in the world do they get these prizes? Last year most of the booths were giving out green and yellow pinwheels and giant combs."

"There must be a giant warehouse somewhere," I said. "It's called 'Ugly Stuff That Nobody Wants,' and they order it by the ton!"

Sonya giggled. "At least let's trade these in for a collector plate. It will be less to carry around, and maybe by the end of the week we can save up enough for a gorilla."

We went back to the water gun booth. Sonya gave the man ten of our mirrors.

He gave her a plastic plate with a picture of the Grand Canyon on it.

We wandered into the exhibition hall to see Sonya's mom. My mother was there now too, stitching away on white satin with white thread. I don't know how she could see what she was doing.

Sonya babbled and bounced for a few minutes, rattling on about our plan to "win" enough Elvis mirrors to trade for Grand Canyon plates to trade for a gorilla.

I threw a helpless look at Mom. I wasn't sure when this had become "our" plan. All I knew was that I used to have six dollars that I traded for six Elvis mirrors. Then Sonya traded five of them and five of hers for one Grand Canyon plate.

Even though I didn't actually want the Elvis mirrors, it somehow seemed better than owning half of a Grand Canyon plate. And I certainly didn't want to own half of a gorilla.

But . . . if Sonya did turn out to be my best friend, it would be perfect to have one gorilla between us. Something we both wanted and worked for together. I decided this might not be a bad plan after all.

Soon there were lots of people carrying Elvis mirrors. They didn't look particularly proud of having spent a dollar for the privilege of walking around with a piece of glass.

That gave Sonya an idea.

The next time she saw a teenager with an Elvis mirror, she stopped him. "Excuse me, but if you don't really want that mirror, could I please have it?"

The guy looked a little surprised at first, then he looked at the mirror and said, "Oh, sure. Here."

I pretended I wasn't with her.

But Sonya was thrilled. "It's a perfect plan, Tabitha. We'll have our gorilla before you know it. Maybe we'll even get two!"

Sonya stood carefully watching everyone's hands as they walked by. Then she saw another Elvis mirror approaching and stepped out to ask for it. Suddenly she shrieked as she saw who was holding it.

"Caitlin!"

"Sonya!" the other girl yelled.

"Oh, Caitlin, I thought you couldn't come. I thought your family was going to Boston."

"We are, but we're not leaving till tomorrow. My dad had to go in to the office today."

"Can you stay overnight? Oh, please? My mom's in here at her basket stand. Let's go ask her."

I moved to follow them, and suddenly Sonya noticed me. "Oh, this is Caitlin, my very best friend in the world." Sonya was smiling and her eyes were sparkling as she wrapped her arm around Caitlin's shoulders.

"She goes to my school and lives in the house right behind me. We do absolutely everything together, and she helps me with the rabbits all the time. She always comes to the fair with me, but this year her family had to go away."

81

I couldn't speak, but they didn't notice.

"Dear Jesus," I prayed under my breath, "please don't let Caitlin spend the night in the camper with us. I don't think I could stand it. My blanky won't get me through this one!"

I followed behind them as they walked, arms wrapped around each other's waist, two blonde heads bobbing and bouncing and sparkling at each other.

What a week this was turning out to be! Sonya already had a best friend, and I had one half of a plastic Grand Canyon plate.

Well, Caitlin didn't get to spend the night, (thank You, Jesus) and I spent all day Tuesday with Sonya. We did the same fun things, and saw everything there was to see, including the trick dogs and the singing magician, about a thousand times. But now that the hope of a best friend was gone, it just wasn't the same. On top of that, Mighty Mouse died.

Mr. Rusk had taken him home, kept him warm, and even tried to get another rabbit to nurse him, but it was just too late. Mighty Mouse didn't have the strength to make it.

I never got a chance to talk to Mom about what happened with Caitlin because Sonya was always there, but I could tell by her eyes that she knew my heart was hurting.

On Wednesday, Mom told me that Grammy was coming over with Mrs.

83

Hanson to baby-sit the cooking exhibits.

While Sonya was in the bathroom, I cornered Mom. "Please, can I go be with Grammy today, without Sonya? I don't have to go through the midway to get to the cooking and sewing building. It's right over there by the tractors. You can see it from here."

So later, Mom said, "Sonya, I'd like you to manage the rabbit house chores this morning without Tabitha. She's going to see her grandmother. Okay?"

And I was off.

Boy, was it good to see Grammy! Her leg was still in a cast, of course, but it didn't seem to bother her at all. And she could really fly on those crutches!

Finally, we got a chance to sit. She listened while I told her everything about Sonya and Caitlin. When I finished, she slowly she opened her eyes and said, "God is good."

I just stared at the floor.

"Tabitha, I've been praying that you would get to know Sonya's inside. Did you?"

84

"Yeah, I guess so. I think she's a lot more beautiful on the outside than on the inside."

"Well, it seems to me that two girls could manage to have a good time at the fair, whether or not they were best friends. Don't let this ruin your week, honey. There's still lots to see and do and learn!"

"Oh, there is, Grammy. Yesterday morning I saw newborn twin baby goats. I mean newborn! They were still wet and could hardly stand up! And I wish you could see the gorilla!"

Grammy's eyebrows shot straight up! "They have a gorilla here?"

"No, not a real one," I laughed. "It's a stuffed animal that's the prize at the water gun game."

I told her how Sonya and I planned to win it.

Grammy frowned. "Let's see. Each time you play, it costs a dollar, and you get one mirror. For each ten mirrors, you get one plate, right?"

85

"Yep," I nodded. "And it only takes five plates to get a gorilla."

"That sounds like fifty dollars to me. You add it up."

"Yes. But, Grammy, we're getting better at shooting the water gun. We may be able to win a plate, and then it won't cost us so much."

"Well, it must be a really terrific gorilla!"

"Oh, it is, Grammy. It is. It's got real-looking shaggy hair and the cutest sad, sleepy eyes. It's worth it. We have two plates and five mirrors already."

"Do you have any money left?"

"I have eight dollars. We don't buy food on the midway 'cause it's too expensive. We eat in the camper. And most of the mirrors we got from asking people. Sonya's so pretty and sweet looking, people just can't say no, I guess."

Grammy hugged me. "You're not so awful looking, yourself, Tabitha."

"Thanks, Grammy," I said. "But it's hard

to feel pretty next to Sonya." Then I said good-bye and headed for lunch.

My morning with Grammy was a nice break from my not-so-nice week. By that afternoon, Sonya and I were ready to face the midway again for Operation Gorilla.

Sonya was very good at asking people for things. She should raise money for charity when she grows up. Not me. I was very good at standing behind her and holding the prizes.

Wednesday and Thursday on the midway got us another collector plate and two extra mirrors. We were getting better at squirting, but still never came close to filling the cup.

And then on Friday we squirted away the last of our money. "Well, that's that, Tabitha," Sonya said. "Let's go back to the camper and add everything up."

On the way back we passed the lady with the trick dogs and the magician. After a week we were pretty bored with them. In fact, by now everything was boring except our one ambition . . . getting a gorilla.

We pulled out the box with our prizes in it.

"Nine, ten, eleven," Sonya counted. "Three plates and eleven mirrors. Let's trade these silly Elvis mirrors in for a plate."

"Great," I said. "We'll have one mirror left over. Then all we need is nine more and we've got a gorilla. Come on."

For the rest of the afternoon, I did my part holding the box with our four plates and one mirror. Sonya asked people for their Elvis mirrors, but this time she didn't have any success. It had rained the night before and everyone was dodging puddles. It was hard to get close enough to people without tripping them.

As bad as I wanted that gorilla, my feet were wet and I was hungry.

"Come on, Sonya. Mom wants us down there for supper. It's getting late."

But it was at supper that things took a turn for the worse. Mom asked how our gorilla project was coming. Sonya looked up casually and said, "Oh, we've given up on that."

88

9

The Strangest Stranger on the Midway

I sure hadn't given up on the gorilla! We were so close! But Sonya signaled me with her eyes not to say anything.

Mom let out her breath. "Well, good. I wasn't really comfortable with you asking people for their prizes anyway. It isn't illegal or anything, but somehow it just didn't seem wise. I'm glad you gave it up."

"Mrs. Bigbee, can Tabitha and I take Mom's supper up to her tonight? We'll be real careful with it, and then we can stay and help her."

"That's a good idea, girls. I wanted to

hang around here tonight and sort of straighten up. Tabitha, Sonya and her mom are staying till Sunday, but you and I and Androcles are leaving in the morning."

She looked at me to see if I were going to protest. I didn't. If Sonya had given up on the gorilla, there was no point in my staying any longer. I sure couldn't get it on my own.

Too bad. It was a really great gorilla.

Mom handed Sonya a plate wrapped in aluminum foil, then she gave me a bag with a soda and silverware in it.

"Here's her supper. It will be getting dark soon, so don't go out on the midway. Stay with Mrs. Strayer. I'll come up later to get you."

Mrs. Strayer was busy with a customer when we got there. So we just set her dinner down on a box behind her table.

"There's your supper, Mom," Sonya said.

Mrs. Strayer looked up and smiled.

Sonya grabbed my arm and pulled me toward the door. When we got outside I noticed she was wearing a canvas bag slung over her shoulder. She pulled it off and opened it up. Inside were our four Grand Canyon plates and the leftover Elvis mirror.

"Now look," she said, "we've got one last chance to get the gorilla."

"I thought you gave up on that. Besides, we're supposed to . . ."

"I just said that, silly. I didn't really mean it. Now do you want the gorilla or not?"

"Yes, but . . ."

"Here's what we do. We only need nine more mirrors. I think if we stand over near the Hammer and the Whirl-A-Way, we'll have better luck. There are a lot of older teenagers over there. They don't want these stupid mirrors, especially if they have to hold them on those fast rides."

"Sonya, it's getting dark."

"Right. But it's not dark yet. So come on. Look, do you want the gorilla? I'll even let

91

you have it first. You can just bring it to the next rabbit meeting. Then it'll be my turn for a month."

I thought about that. This was the first time we had talked about exactly how we were going to share the gorilla. It really wasn't a bad plan.

She pressed me for an answer. "Well? I don't know what your problem is. I'm doing all the work! If you don't come with me, I'll just do it myself, and the gorilla will be mine."

She turned around in a flounce, and walked away toward a group of teenage boys, smoking next to the Whirl-A-Way.

I followed her.

Sonya's plan was a good one. We got a few mirrors right away. But I didn't like the midway after dark. Everything seemed bigger and louder and ruder than in the daylight. Funny, but all week long I'd hardly noticed people screaming on the rides. But in the dark it was scary.

Hopefully we'd get the mirrors we needed, and get out of there.

"Excuse me, Mister," Sonya said to a tall man eating a piece of pizza. "Do you really want that dumb Elvis mirror?"

The man swallowed a mouthful of pizza, laughed, and wiped at some sauce that had dripped onto his white T-shirt. "No, do you? Here, you can have it! I can't eat and hang onto that thing anyway. What a mess!"

Sonya smiled her best twinkly smile. "Thanks a lot, mister. We only need five more. Then we're getting a gorilla!"

The man looked interested. "Are you really? Well I just came from there. There's only one gorilla left."

He finished up his pizza and wiped his mouth. "You might have to settle for a pink pony or whatever else they'll throw at you this late in the week."

I tugged at Sonya's arm. "What are we going to do? If we can't get more mirrors in a hurry, it'll be gone!"

93

We started walking toward the water gun game, and the man walked alongside us.

"You know," he said, "these games are all rigged. Take those water guns for instance. You think it's to your advantage that the cups are tilted toward you. But actually that just keeps you from bouncing the water off the wall and into the cup."

Sonya nodded. "Yeah. And most of the water splashes right back out." By then we were at the game.

"Well, look," the man said, "I'd like to try this again and see if I can beat it. Stick around. If I don't do it, I'll at least get a few more of those valuable mirrors. How many did you say you needed?"

"Five!" we both said at the same time.

The man paid his dollar, and sat down at the booth. "Okay, pay close attention," he laughed. "You may get to see an expert at work. Then again, maybe you won't."

We crowded up behind him to watch. The bell rang, and he began to fire. But when the bell rang again and the water shut off, the cup was only half full.

He handed his mirror to Sonya, and she put it in her canvas bag. The man rubbed his chin a minute, winked at me, and tugged on Sonya's hair.

"Okay, my sweeties. I may not be an expert, but I never give up! Let's get something to drink, and then we'll try again."

He bought us all orange sodas and paid another dollar at the water-gun game.

Three more dollars followed that one, and the man triumphantly handed us our last mirror. Then he turned to the man who ran the game.

"My little girls here have some mirrors to trade in." We exchanged them for a Grand Canyon plate. I never thought such an ugly plate would look so good.

"And now," said the man, rubbing his hands together and wiping them on his jeans, "the moment you've all been waiting for. . . ."

He took the five plastic plates and pre-
sented them in grand fashion to the man at
the booth. "One gorilla, please!"

Wow! We actually did it! Sonya and I
hugged the gorilla between us. Even if she
wasn't my best friend, having this gorilla
gave us something special to share, and
that was worth it.

We thanked the man for helping us and

walked away. "Wait till Mom sees this. She didn't think we could do it," I said.

But then I realized that the man was still with us. Maybe he was waiting to be properly appreciated. I took the gorilla from Sonya and turned around.

"Thanks again, Mister. We really couldn't have gotten this without your help. And thanks for the drinks. It was very nice of you." We started to walk away again.

The man came up between us and put one arm around each of our shoulders.

"Oh, don't worry about it, girls. I'm sure we can work something out."

I didn't like the sound of that. "What do you mean, 'work something out'?" I asked, trying to make my voice sound very strong.

"I mean," said the man, leaning down close to our ears, "you owe me for the gorilla and the drinks. But I'm sure we can find a way for you to pay me back."

Alarm bells rang in my head. That line was straight out of our stranger awareness

97

program at school. I started to pull away, but now the man was holding tightly onto the hair at the back of my neck, and to Sonya's too, from the look on her face.

But to everyone who passed us, he just looked like a man with two daughters. They couldn't tell we couldn't get away.

"Don't try to scream," he said, "and you won't get hurt."

No one could have heard us if we had screamed, anyway. We were right next to the Whirl-A-Way now, where the noise was incredible. He was leading us around behind the rides, where there weren't any people. Just trucks and machines—and darkness.

If we didn't get away right now . . .

·10·

The Biggest Dope on the Face of the Earth

I caught Sonya's eye, and doubled up my fist to show her we had to fight, even if we got hurt.

I silently mouthed the words, "One! Two! Three!"

On three, I grabbed the gorilla by one arm and whacked it into the man's face as hard as I could, then I stomped on his foot. Sonya threw the rest of her soda at him and crammed her elbow into him with all her might.

He doubled over, clutching himself with his left hand and trying to get his right hand untangled from my hair. I ripped it free, and hollered, "RUN!"

Sonya reached out for my hand and we flew through the crowd, knocking into people on every side, and made it to the exhibition hall.

We absolutely threw ourselves behind Mrs. Strayer's basket table, nearly knocking it over.

She turned around in a flurry to scold us, but by then we had dissolved in a flood of tears in each other's arms.

Dad almost ran up to the police sergeant's desk. "I'm Richard Bigbee. Where? . . ."

The officer pointed across the room to where we were sitting.

"Tabitha!" Daddy was shaking all over and fighting back the tears. I hate it when daddies cry. "Are you all right, sweetie?"

It was at least the sixteenth time that someone had asked if I were all right, but I didn't mind. I nodded and hugged Daddy's chest for a long time.

He looked around. "Where's Sonya?"

Mom answered him. "She and her parents are in there giving a statement. They wanted to talk to the girls separately."

I had already been through all the "what exactly did he look like?" "what exactly did he say?" and "where exactly did he touch you?" questions, so I knew what was happening to Sonya. I wish they had let us go in together.

"I just want to know one thing," Daddy asked. "What were you doing out on the midway in the first place?"

But Mom put her hand on his arm. "Can we do that later, honey? Tabitha needs to think this through by herself first. Right now, let's just praise God that she's okay."

Dad settled down, pulled me onto his lap, and rocked me a little, like I was a baby.

I knew all the things he wanted to say to me. I was his baby. And why couldn't I obey a simple rule? And was a stupid gorilla really all that important?

I had been asking myself those same questions all the way to the police station.

The stupid gorilla had disappeared in the fight anyway. Someone probably picked it up off the ground on the midway and took it home. Well, they could have it! I just hope it didn't cause any more trouble.

The Strayers finally came out.

The policeman talked to us all. "Well, folks, these are two very lucky little girls. That man has been following the fair all over the state. At every town we get reports, after the fact, from other kids who weren't so lucky. But we could never catch him. Till now."

Dad looked up. "Then you've got him?"

The officer gave us a funny little smile. "Yes, well, you see, the culprit was in such pain after you girls left him, a security officer stopped to help him. When he acted scared and refused help, the guard got suspicious and took him to the security office to call us.

"Well, just then Mrs. Strayer's call came in. We told security to look for a tall man with pizza on a white T-shirt. The guard on the phone was sitting there looking straight at him.

"It's a good thing you acted so fast, all of you. You've saved other kids a lot of pain and heartache.

"Now, girls, I know you're going to get this same lecture at home, but I'm giving it to you here too.

"You did the right thing, once you knew you were in trouble. But never get that close to trouble again. Things like that happen even in broad daylight. That man, and others like him, can be very nice-looking, and they seem kind, generous, and friendly at first. But that's just on the surface. Down inside they're evil."

After my talk with Grammy, I had been thinking that Sonya was a lot less beautiful on the inside than on the outside, but this man who tried to hurt us was the absolute winner in the beautiful outside/ugly inside category. Grammy said that God loves all of us, even though He can see how ugly our insides are. Could He love someone with an inside as ugly as that man's? I'd have to ask Grammy about that.

The policeman went on to repeat our entire stranger awareness unit. But I didn't mind listening this time. Never again would I be so caught up in wanting something that I would disobey and take chances.

I slept that night at home in my own bed. Well, part of the night. After everyone else was asleep, I crept downstairs to Grammy's room.

"Grammy," I whispered. I wasn't sure if she heard me. "Grammy, would it hurt your leg if I got in your bed?"

"Not at all," she whispered back. "This

bed is plenty big enough for two."

I climbed in and settled down under the covers.

"Gram, God loves everybody, right?"

"Right," Grammy answered.

"Even . . . " I couldn't finish.

There was silence for a moment. "Yes, even him," she answered. "God hates how that man acted, and will see that he is punished. But He still loves him . . . enough to die for him. Now go to sleep, sweetie. We'll talk about this later."

The next morning, Dad drove me back to the fair to get our things, and Androcles, of course.

Dad picked up her chicken crate and went out to put her in the car.

I wandered around to Dopey's hutch. "Look at you," I said to the pretty little rabbit. "You've chewed your ribbon. That says 'Best of Breed,' not 'Best to Eat'!" I moved the ribbon where he couldn't reach it through the wire.

"You know, I always thought you were too fine a rabbit for such a silly name. Dopey! I'm the only one around here who's dopey!

"A classy Polish rabbit should have a classy Polish name. I used to know a Polish man named Reverend Kruscinski. He was very classy and very educated. From now on, you can call me Dopey, and I'll call you Reverend Dopinski. Or maybe just Dopinski. But you'd better not tell Sonya."

"Tell me what?"

I turned around and blushed, because there was Sonya standing at the door.

"Oh, hi. I'm sorry. I was just telling Dopey that he deserved a really important-sounding name, now that he's won a ribbon."

"Like what?"

"How about Dopinski? It's a proper Polish name."

Sonya giggled. "That's great! I like it. Thanks . . . and uh . . . you know, Tabitha, I'm

106

really sorry about . . . well, about all the trouble we got into. I should have listened to you."

"Well, I knew better. But even though it was wrong to go, I'm glad I didn't let you go by yourself. You might not have had a chance against him alone."

"Thank you," she said, looking at the floor.

I didn't really know what else to say. Suddenly Sonya flashed me a brilliant smile, spun around and hollered over her shoulder, " 'Bye. See you at the next club meeting."

I wasn't sure I was going to be at the next rabbit club meeting. I just wanted to get home to my family, and my new back porch. I just wanted to take care of Androcles in her own pen, practice on my skateboard with Jason, and try to crank myself up for school to start on Tuesday.

"Good-bye, Dopinski."

I got into the car and Dad took off. But he didn't head for the gate. Instead he drove up around to the parking lot by the midway.

"Don't ask any questions, Tabitha. Just come with me. There's one more thing we have to do."

I walked with Daddy through the midway. He stopped at the water gun booth. Without saying a word, or even looking at me, Daddy paid the man a dollar, and sat down at a gun.

What in the world was he doing? I had never seen my father play one of these games before. I hoped he didn't think he had to win me a gorilla. There weren't any left, anyway.

Daddy squirted right at the cup, and most of the water splashed right back out. The bell rang, and the game was over.

Daddy collected his Elvis mirror and held it out to me. "This is to hang in your room, Tabitha. So you never forget. I love you more than life itself, sweetheart. I die inside when I think of what would have happened to you if the Lord had not been right at your side. Praise God you're okay. Now let's go home."

I could hardly see, because of my tears. I would hang this on the wall beside my bed. Funny to think that a picture of Elvis Presley could remind me of God's love and my father's love. But this one always would.

It was actually kind of ugly—on the outside—but what it meant to me was the most beautiful thing in the world.

I settled down beside Androcles. Her

chicken crate hung out over the edge of the backseat, and was propped up against the back of the driver's seat by sleeping bags and a suitcase.

Dad turned around as he started the car.

"Tabitha, if you ever need to talk about better ways to protect yourself, or about where things went wrong with Sonya, you know that Mom and I are here to help you."

A flood of shame came over me, all over again. I know I got myself into that mess by disobeying and by being greedy and by not standing up to Sonya. What else was there to talk about?

I looked up through my tears. "I'm sorry, Daddy."

He faced the front and started the car. "Well, I hope you are. And from now on, just remember one thing . . . "

I braced myself for what he was going to say.

"I forgive you, Tabitha."

"Really, Daddy?"

"Really, totally, completely. And I love you."

I hauled myself across in front of Androcles and kissed the back of Daddy's neck.

Then I flopped back down and fastened my seat belt. I closed my eyes. "I'm sorry, Jesus," I whispered. "I've been very stupid and selfish. Could You please forgive me, and help me to obey from now on?"

I didn't talk at all the rest of the way home. I just sat there, stroking Androcles through the cage, and feeling better and better as we got closer to home.

When you were the biggest dope on the face of the earth, it felt good to be forgiven.